P9-DGR-138

HENRY COLE

Nesting

Katherine Tegen Books

An Imprint of HarperCollins Publishers

It is an early spring morning.
The ground is covered with frost.
From the branch of an apple tree,
a robin starts to sing.

His song tells other male robins,
"Stay away!"
But a female hears his song, too.
"Here I am!" he sings.

The two robins explore. One spot looks perfect.
Together they gather dry grass and small twigs.

They begin to build a nest.

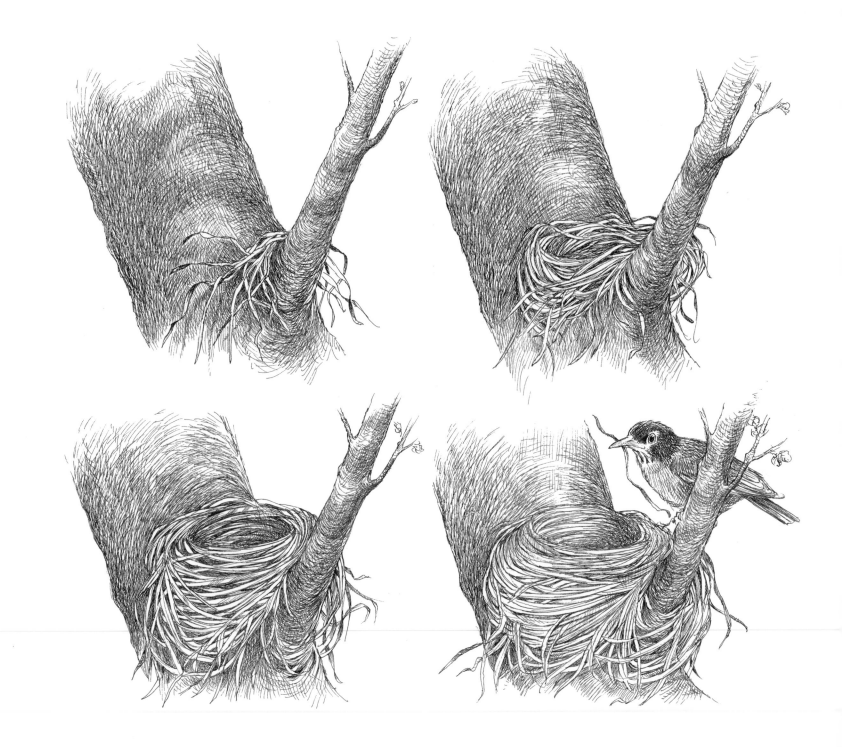

The nest is finished.

It is perfect.

It is just the the right size and shape.

The mother robin settles into it and sits quietly.

She lays an egg.
It is smooth and blue.

She lays three more.

Four is perfect.

She keeps the eggs warm.

She is patient.

Inside each egg, a baby bird is growing.

The eggs begin to hatch, one by one.

The babies have no feathers. They are blind and defenseless.

And very hungry.
A juicy caterpillar is a perfect meal
for baby robins. So is a soft worm.

One afternoon, a storm comes!

The wind blows and rain pours.

The babies are kept safe.

The storm passes.

Day after day, the babies need more food.

The parents make many, many trips.

Down below, a snake sees the robins' nest.
The snake is hungry, too, and climbs
the apple tree.

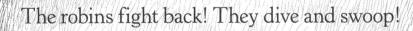

The robins fight back! They dive and swoop!

They don't give up until they drive the snake away.

The young robins have grown bigger and bigger.

They fill up the nest!

They have feathers now, just right for flying.

One by one they leave the nest.
They flap and flap and drop
to the ground below.

Soon they grow strong and can feed themselves.
Their wings take them anywhere they want to go.

It is late summer now, and the days are shorter.

The robins eat berries and grow fat.

Now they can survive a cold winter.

They gather to spend the winter months together.

The old nest is covered with snow.
A new nest will take its place when
spring comes again.

AUTHOR'S NOTE

- American robins can be found in backyards and gardens all across North America. The male robin's cheerful song is one of the first signs announcing that spring has arrived.

- Usually robins build nests in trees or shrubs, but they also use eaves of buildings, gutters, porches of houses, or the tops of outdoor light fixtures. The female does most of the nest building, using twigs and grass. She adds mud to make it strong.

- Then the female robin lays eggs. Four eggs are most common. She incubates the eggs for about two weeks, keeping them warm so the chicks can grow and develop inside.

- When the eggs hatch, the baby robins are blind and have no feathers. But they are fed by the parent robins for another two weeks or so, until at last they grow big and have enough feathers to fly.

- It's tough to be a robin. They have many predators. The robins that live past their first year are strong. They have learned how to survive.

Library of Congress Cataloging-in-Publication Data

Names: Cole, Henry, author, illustrator.
Title: Nesting / Henry Cole.
Description: First edition. | New York, NY : Katherine Tegen Books, an imprint of HarperCollins Publishers, [2019] | Summary: A pair of robins
    build a nest together and raise their chicks, navigating a year of changing seasons and serpentine predators.
Identifiers: LCCN 2019000075 | ISBN 9780062885920 (hardcover)
Subjects: LCSH: Robins—Juvenile fiction. | CYAC: Robins—Fiction. | Birds—Nests—Fiction. | Nature—Fiction.
Classification: LCC PZ10.3.C6839 Ne 2019 | DDC [E]--dc23 LC record available at https://lccn.loc.gov/2019000075

The artist used Micron pens and acrylic paints to create the illustrations for this book. Typography by Dana Fritts and Andrea Vandergrift 19 20 21 22 23 SCP 10 9 8 7 6 5 4 3 2 1
❖
First Edition